Mrs. Brown Went to Town

by Wong Herbert Yee

Houghton Mifflin Company

Boston

www.houghtonmifflinbooks.com

Typography by Ariel Apte
The text of this book is set in 17-point Giovanni.
The illustrations are watercolor, reproduced in full color.

Library of Congress Cataloging-in-Publication Data
Yee, Wong Herbert.
Mrs. Brown went to town / Wong Herbert Yee.
p. cm.
Summary: When Mrs. Brown goes to the hospital, her farm animals—
a cow, two pigs, three ducks, and a yak—take over her house.
Hardcover ISBN 0-395-75282-5 Paperback ISBN 0-618-36918-X
[Domestic animals—Fiction. 2. Stories in rhyme.] I. Title.
PZ8.3.Y42Mr 1996
[E]—dc20 95-23389 CIP AC

Manufactured in China

SCP 10 9 8 7 6 5 4

For Moon Angel

Mrs. Brown lives in the barn out back
With a cow, two pigs, three ducks, and a yak.
Life on the farm wasn't always this way.
Everything changed just last Saturday.

When riding her bicycle down the street,
A terrier tasted Mrs. Brown's feet.

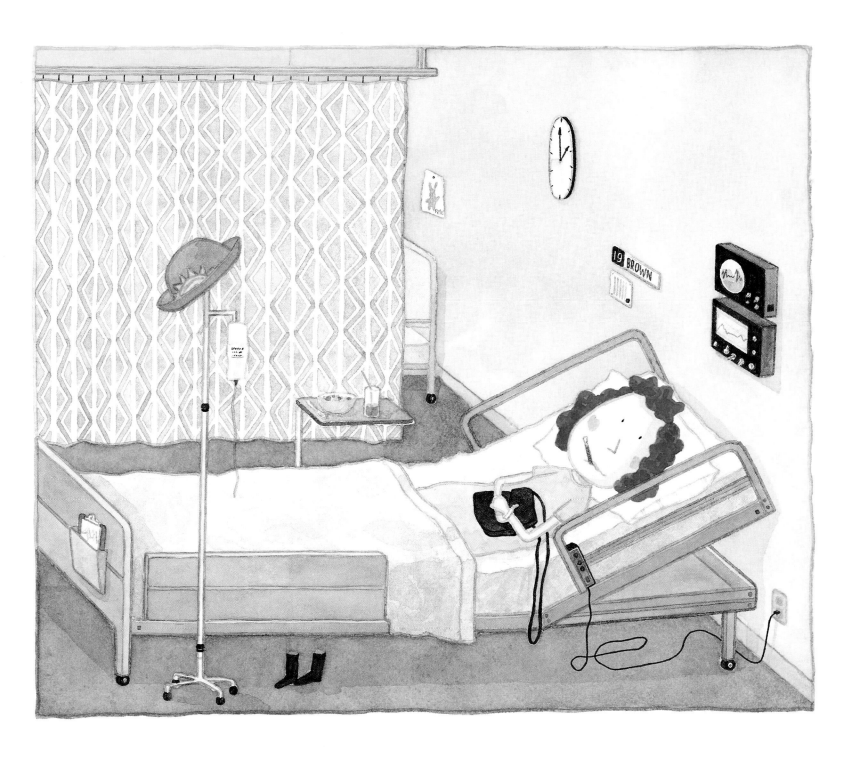

In a hospital bed she rested,
Waiting to be x-rayed and tested.

Mrs. Brown sent word in a letter

To say she'd come home, when she was better.

The postman delivered the letter out back

For a cow, two pigs, three ducks, and a yak.

All the animals, except for a mouse,
Voted to move into Mrs. Brown's house.

They rang the doorbell
To hear the chimes,

Flushed the toilet
One hundred times,

Raced up the stairs, came sliding back down,
Each one wearing a different gown,

Took turns bouncing on Mrs. Brown's bed,

Painted the house in matching barn red.

They raided the pantry,
Prepared a snack
For a cow, two pigs,
Three ducks, and a yak.

In the bathroom they played for hours
Putting on makeup and taking long showers.

They dried off in front of a roaring fire,
Warm and cozy but beginning to tire,

Tiptoed upstairs by candlelight,
Borrowed pajamas to wear for the night.

The hospital released Mrs. Brown at eight.
A taxicab dropped her off by the gate.

She hobbled upstairs and crawled in the sack
Didn't see a cow, two pigs, three ducks, and a yak.

The floor beneath them began to quake.
The walls and windows started to shake.
All this commotion woke Mrs. Brown
In time to feel her bed crashing down!

The police were first to arrive on the scene.
Fire trucks dispatched from station thirteen.

An ambulance raced all the way from town
And carried away poor Mrs. Brown.

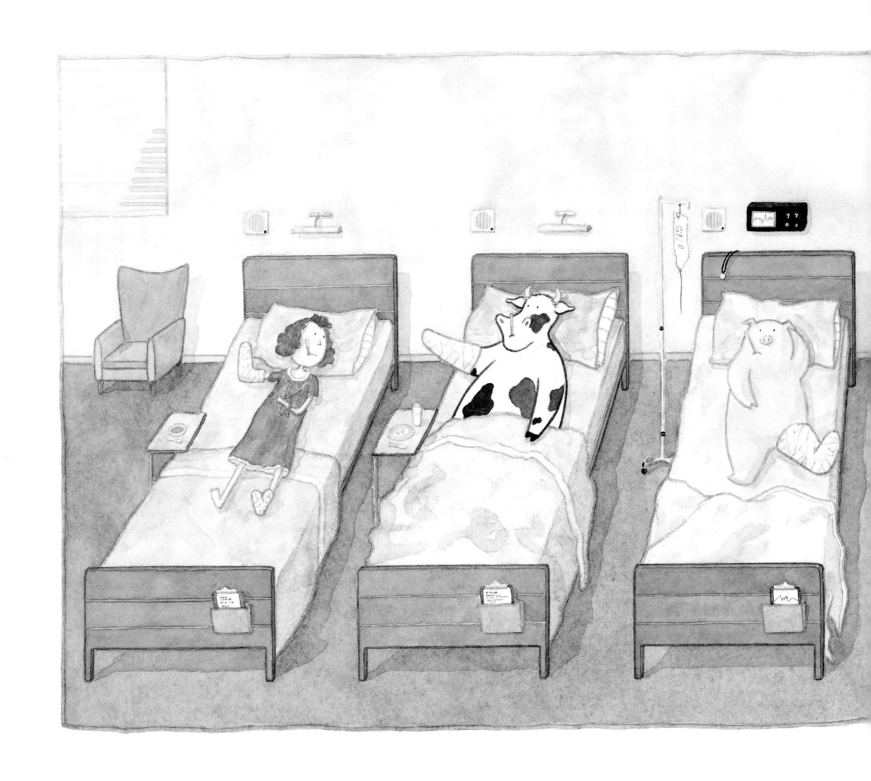

In the hospital she lay on her back

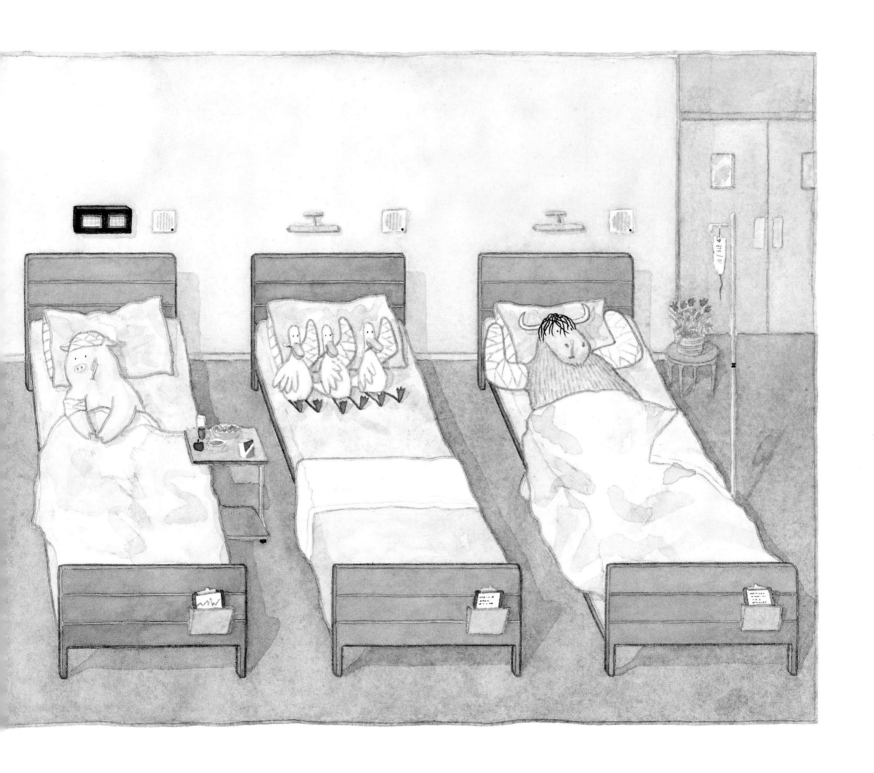

With a cow, two pigs, three ducks, and a yak.

The hospital released Mrs. Brown at ten.
The doctors waved good-bye once again.

Into a taxi they crammed all eight.
The driver dropped them off by the gate.
He swept out the feathers and hair
And charged Mrs. Brown twice the fare.

Life on the farm wasn't always this way
Until Mrs. Brown went to town that day.
So now she lives in the barn out back
With a cow, two pigs, three ducks, and a yak.